Childrens Poems and Rhymes

by
Gula Palmer

illustration
Teresa Ferracci

Gula Palmer
2073 West Hedding Street
San Jose, CA 95128

ISBN 978-0-615-15758-0
Library of Congress Control Number: 2007910299
Copyright © 2008 by Gula Palmer
All Rights Reserved. Self published by Gula Palmer.

First printing, January 2008
Printed in China

Cover art and all illustrations done by Teresa Ferracci

I would like to dedicate my book to my three children,

Michele, Bob, and Tim,

Also to my grandchildren,

Kristjan, Perry, Collin, Nicholas, Shayne, Scott and Stacy,

who are the loves of my Life.

I also want to thank my wonderful mate, Gene,

for being so patient and understanding.

A Special dedication to all the hundreds of children that I had

the pleasure of teaching over the past 35 years

and their parents.

Childrens Poems and Rhymes

TO THE CHILDREN
OF THE WORLD

May each child in the World, know happines and love,

And each day bring them a rainbow from above,

May they start each day with a smile on their face,

And let them always feel like they have won first place.

May they sleep each night in their own warm beds,

And always have a loving roof over their heads.

In this world of war and peace, may they never have to

choose any decision that would make them lose

That special time in each childs life,

That fills their hearts with much delight.

THE SEA SHELL

I wish I were a seashell,
That lived out in the sea.
I'd live below the water,
And the fish would play
With me.

The waves would
Polish me up
Real bright,
Then, folks would find me
With much delight.

BLUEBIRDS

There were two little bluebirds

In their nest.

Each vowed to the other that

He loved the best.

But the truth of the matter,

If they only knew,

Was that each of their love

Was what you call "true blue".

THE GRASSHOPPER

Have you ever held a grasshopper
In the palm of your hand,
Then watched as he jumped up
And found a place to land?
They have two big feelers
On the top of their head
And sometimes don't move
And pretend to be dead.
But even if a small noise is made,
They will quickly jump
And hide away.

LADYBUG

I am a little ladybug and I'm cute as I can be.
I sniff among the flowers
And fly around for hours.
I am a very pretty red,
with little feelers on my head.
You can hold me in your
Hand real tight,
Because I never,
Ever bite,
Then let me fly away.

MY
BLUE JAY

There once lived
A little blue jay,
She sat high up in my tree.
Each and every morning,
She would sing sweet songs to me.

She loved for me to feed
Her bread,
But she would never, ever,
Let me pat her on the
head.

My Doll

I had a little doll,
And Violet
Was her name.
She brought me lots
Of happiness
While playing many games.

She could walk, she could talk,
And she could move
Her little head.
She always cuddled
Up to me
When we crawled
Into bed.

THE PINE TREE

I am a pine tree,
Tall and strong.
I stand in the woods
All year long.
The wind makes my branches
Swing and sway,
Especially on a stormy day.

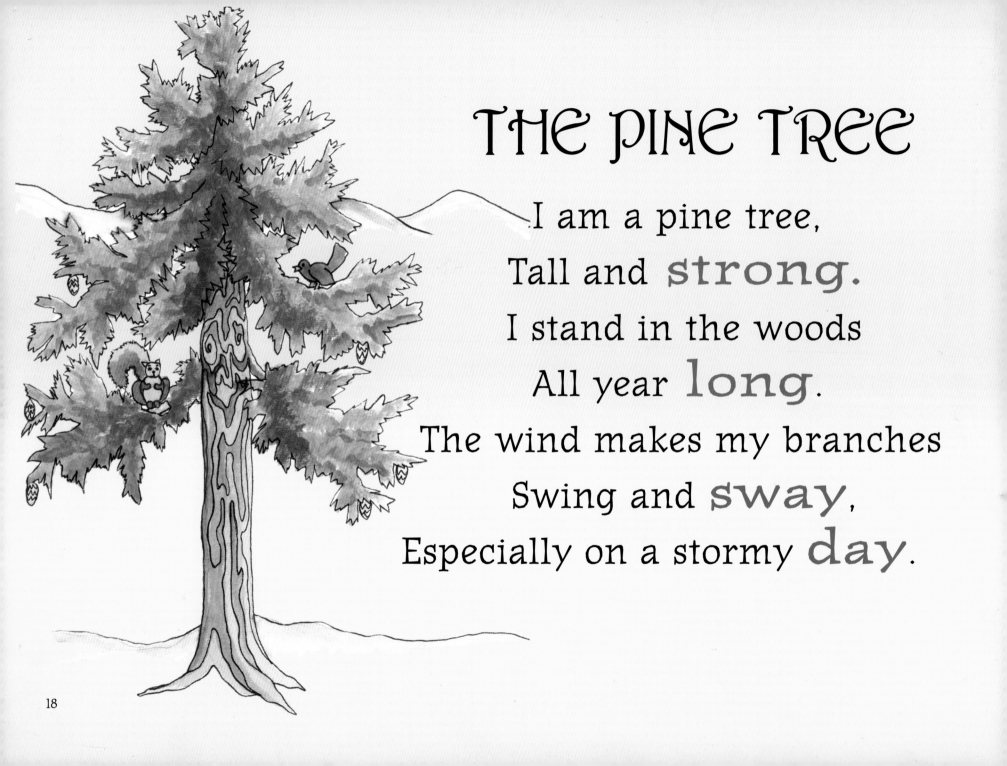

The birds and squirrels just love to play
Among my branches ever day.
If I could talk, I know what
I would say,

"Please take a walk
In the woods today."

THE HILL

I love to climb the hill so high,
Sit on the top And watch the clouds roll by-
One shaped like a cat,
One shaped like a dog,
And, oh my gosh, there's one
Shaped like a frog!

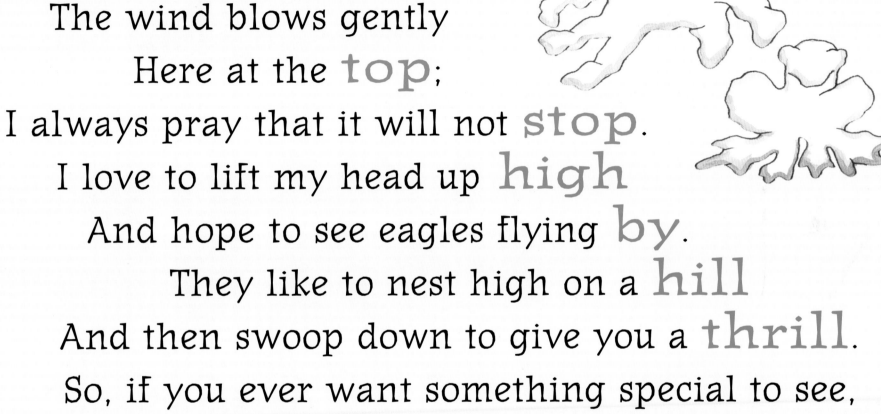

The wind blows gently
Here at the top;
I always pray that it will not stop.
I love to lift my head up high
And hope to see eagles flying by.
They like to nest high on a hill
And then swoop down to give you a thrill.
So, if you ever want something special to see,

Please, come and
climb a hill with me.

THE FARM

It is so much fun to be on a farm,
Especially when you play in the barn.
I like to climb to the hayloft high
And gaze outside at the Light blue sky.
Then, I romp around in all the hay
And figure out lots of Games to play.

22

THE COW

There once lived a cow named Nash.
He loved to eat green
grass.
He would moo all
day,
Then sleep in the
hay.
And that's the tale of
Nash.

BASKETBALL

Basketball was his game
And Robert was his name.
He loved to shoot and run
Because it was so much fun.
Hour after hour,
You could watch
Him with his power.

Always there and always fair,
Whether he won or lost
He would never be cross.
He just loved to play
the game,
And never needed
Any fame.

MY FLOWERS

Blue, yellow, and white flowers are my delight.
I plant them in the early spring
While listening to the robins sing.

The sun shines bright and helps them grow
And soon the whole wide world will know
The joy that every flower brings
Each and every early spring.

MY FRIEND KATE

I had a friend and her name was Kate.
Boy, she loved to roller skate.
Glide to the left, glide to the right,
She would take my hand and
Hold on tight,
Then spin me around
With all her might.

Wow!
What a fright!

THE RAIN

I like to go outside and play,
Especially on a rainy day.
I splash in puddles large and small
And always hope that I won't fall.
The wonderful smell that fresh rain brings
Reminds me of many special things,
Like fallen leaves and
Fresh green grass.
I always hoped the rain
Would last.

KING AND QUEEN

There once lived a queen and
king
And they both loved to
sing.

She sang high
And he sung low,
But neither one
Could sing solo.

ALAS, WHAT
A SHAME!

THE LEAVES

Have you ever walked among the leaves
On a lovely winter day?
Have you ever seen the colors,
Orange and brown,
Floating down upon the
ground?

I love to run and kick them high
And watch them float
Up towards the sky.
Please, come with me
And have some fun,
While we take a walk
In the nice warm sun.

THE SWING

I am a swing
Made of rope and wood
And I hang in a big oak
tree.
Lots and lots of children like
To take a ride on me.

I swing them low
And I swing them
high,
So they can see the cool blue sky.
Don't be afraid and try to hide,
Just drop by me and take a ride.

THE FOUR REGIONS

North, South, East, West,
Which one do you like the best?

The sun rises in the east
And sets in the west.

The south is nice and
warm,
And the north has lots of
storms.
But whichever one you
choose,
You will never, ever
lose,
Because each of our four
regions
Has its own special
seasons.

THE BEAR

There once was a bear
And her name was Mary.
She lived in the woods
And ate lots of berries.
She would bask in the sun
From morning till noon,
Then roam through the woods
Looking for room
To make her bed,
So she could rest her little head.

THE KITE

I once had a kite
And much to my
delight
It would fly real
high, way up in the sky.
Then the wind would blow,
Causing my kite to flow –

Up and down and all around,
But never touching upon the
ground.
It is always such a sight
For anyone who
Flies a kite.

MULBERRY TREE

There once lived a
Squirrel, a mouse,
And a rat named Dee,
And they all ran around
My mulberry tree.
One ran up
And one ran down,
While the one remaining

42

Sat on the ground.
They would have such fun,
Especially in the sun,
But at the end of the day
They would stop their play.

WHAT
A SHAME!

LITTLE GRAY MOUSE

There once
Lived a little
Gray
mouse
Who lived in
A tiny house.

44

He loved to go out and play
Except on a rainy day.
He would sit and twist his whiskers
And chase his little sisters
Out and in and in and out,
Until his mother gave a great big shout.

"GET OUT!"

MY FATHER

My father brought me roses
And he picked them just for
me.
He bought me lovely presents
For everyone to
see.

But the greatest

Gift he ever gave

WAS ALL
HIS
LOVE TO
ME.

THE SNAKE

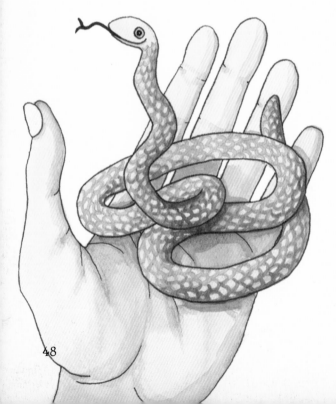

I had a little green snake
And his name was Jake.
He liked to curl up in my hand,
And then lift up tall to stand.
He made a little hissing sound
And loved to crawl
Upon the ground.
I would place him
In his cage each night;
He seemed to feel
It was all quite right.

MY DONKEY

I had a little donkey
And Billie was his name.
He gave me rides to market
And never did complain.
He liked to stand
Beneath the tree,
And always kept
His eyes on me.
What a wonderful
Friend he was to me.

THE LITTLE MERMAID

I am a little mermaid and
I'm cute as I can be.
I live deep in the ocean and the
Fish all play with me.
My tail flips up
And then flips
down,

50

And keeps me swimming
All around.
So if you ever go swimming
In the sea,
You might be lucky, and
Get to play with me.

MY PONY

I had a pretty pony;
She was sweet as she could be.
She loved to romp across the ground
And run straight back to me.
She had a lovely yellow mane,
And would always come
When I called her name.

A pony is always
Such a sight,
And will always
Bring you
Much delight

MR. GOAT

There once lived a goat
Named Bill.
He liked to graze
On the hill.
He would chew the
grass
And run real
fast –

Up and down,
And down and up.

And never,
never would
he fill up!

THE LITTLE SKUNK

There once lived a skunk
Named Dale.
He had a beautiful fluffy tail.
He loved to spend his hours
Smelling all the forest
flowers.

Then through the woods
He would roam,
But never, never
Strayed far
From
home.

SIX PIGS

Two, four, six little pigs
All of them trying to learn to do the jig -

Two to the left and two to the right,
And two jumped around with all their might.
What a thrill it was for me
to see
Six little pigs
Learning to do
The jig.

LITTLE DUCK

I had a little baby duck;
He was cute as he could be.

He loved to
Jump into my
Tub
And take a bath
With me.
His feet were
Webbed

And his beak was brown,
And you could
Hear him
Quack all over
town.

Wow!
What a
noise!

SPIDER MONKEY

I am a spider monkey,
And I'm cute as I can be.
Lots and lots of people
Try to mimic me.
They feed me fruit
and peanuts, too.
Then, I like to play
peek-a-boo.

62

I pop out, and I pop in,
And they just watch
and give me a grin.

What a
game I play!

THE PARK

I like to walk in the park each day.
It is so much fun to see
The children at play,
Two on the seesaw
Going up and down,
Boys playing marbles
On the ground.

A little girl
Going down a slide,
Two young boys
On a swing flying high,
There are always so many things to see.
So please, take a walk in the park
With me.

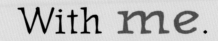

LITTLE
RED HEN

Once upon a time there
Lived a little red hen.
She lived her life
In a very nice pen.
She would ruffle her
Feathers and strut all
around,

CHICKENS' ROOST

While scratching her
Feet on the nice soft
ground.
But she would
Quickly fly away
When the kids
came out to play.

THE SNOWFLAKE

I am a snowflake,
Fluffy and white.
I shine like a diamond,
Especially at night.
Children love to play
In my snow each day
And hope that I won't fly away.

They glide their sleds up and
Down hills;
It always gives them
Such a thrill.
So, when you see me
Floating down,
Don't try to pick me up off
The ground.

For I will melt.

MY ROBIN

There was a little robin
She was sweet
As she could be.
She loved to fly around
My yard and sing sweet
Songs to me.

She built a nest in my lime tree
And shared her baby birds
With me.
The day would come
When they had to go
But until that day,
I loved them so.

71

HAPPY CLOWN

It's lots of fun to be a clown
You try to help people
From feeling down.
I wear a very colorful suit,
With my face painted up
To look real cute.

72

My smile goes up
And never down,
And that's why I'm known
As the happy clown.

A RAINBOW

A rainbow is God's masterpiece

For all the world to see -

Especially you and me.

When it's raining and you're feeling blue

God sends his rainbow shining through.

Its many colors glowing bright

Will always bring you much delight.

In all this land of worldly things,

If you owned a rainbow you would be king.

The
End